Y0-AUZ-961

In Confidence

West Orange Public Library

" The Maria Mazziotti Gillan
Poetry Collection"

Donated by
Frank Niccoletti

In Confidence

poems by

Jim Tilley

WEST ORANGE PUBLIC LIBRARY
46 MT. PLEASANT AVE.
WEST ORANGE, NJ 07052
10/13

RED HEN PRESS | Pasadena, California

In Confidence

Copyright © 2011 by Jim Tilley

All rights reserved

No part of this book may be used or reproduced in any manner whatsoever without the prior written permission of both the publisher and the copyright owner.

Book design by Mark E. Cull
Book layout by Kathrine Davidson
Cover artwork by Leslie J. Freeman
Author photo by Deborah C. Schneider

ISBN: 978-1-59709-473-3 (tradepaper)
ISBN: 978-1-59709-109-1 (clothbound)
Library of Congress Data
Tilley, Jim.
In confidence : poems / by Jim Tilley.—1st ed.
p. cm.
I. Title.
PS3620.I515I6 2011
811'.6—dc22

2010042938

The Los Angeles County Arts Commission, the California Arts Council, the National Endowment for the Arts, and Los Angeles Department of Cultural Affairs partially support Red Hen Press.

Published by Red Hen Press
www.redhen.org
First Edition

Acknowledgments

Grateful acknowledgment is made to the following journals in which certain of the poems in this book first appeared, sometimes under different titles or in previous versions. *Atlanta Review,* "One Would Hope"; *Baltimore Review,* "Aluminum Rush"; *Chattahoochee Review,* "Slaying Philistines"; *Cortland Review (online),* "Fish at the Dance"; *Florida Review,* "A Belated Calculus," "Vocabulary Test"; *Free Lunch,* "Gradients"; *Hawai'i Review,* "Things Not Asked"; *Hurricane Review,* "Chemotherapy," "Not Yet," "The Breakers"; *New Delta Review,* "In Spring, Mathematics Are Yellow"; *Rattle,* "Folding"; *Red Cedar Review,* "After Wine"; *Rhino,* "Serendipity in the Cosmos"; *Southern Poetry Review,* "Half-Finished Bridge"; *Southern Review,* "In Confidence"; *Sou'wester,* "Rehearsal"; *Sycamore Review,* "Murmur," "On the Art of Patience"; *Tar River Poetry,* "Richter 7.8"; *Tusculum Review (online),* "Binoculars," "From the Forest Comes the Call," "Something Missing," "The Ivy and the Brick," "The Clay and the Fire," "Variations on a Theme by Yeats."

The six poems appearing on *The Tusculum Review's* Website were published as part of their Featured Artist series.

"On the Art of Patience" won *Sycamore Review*'s Wabash Prize.

"Binoculars" won the New England Poetry Club's Firman Houghton Award.

"Serendipity in the Cosmos" was a *Rhino* editors' choice as best poem and was nominated for a Pushcart Prize.

"Rehearsal," "On the Art of Patience," and "Richter 7.8" were nominated for a Pushcart Prize.

"On the Art of Patience," "Half-Finished Bridge," and "One Would Hope" also appear in the online *Enskyment Anthology*.

"Richter 7.8" also appears in "Literature to Go" (*Bedford/St. Martin's*), edited by Michael Meyer.

I want to thank several of my artist and poet friends for their assistance: Jim Scruton, who critiqued the full manuscript and suggested the Whitman epigraph; Charlie Coté, who tirelessly reviews all my work; Bill Shelton and Cindy Mallard, whom I can always count on for unvarnished views about my writing; and Leslie Freeman, who not only commented on several of the book's poems but also conceived and painted the art for the book's cover.

A special thanks to Heather Mitchell, who, through a friend, introduced me to Kate Gale, co-founder and managing editor of Red Hen Press, and to Kate and her husband, Mark Cull, who have made the production of this book possible.

Above all, I want to thank my wife, Deborah Schneider. She has been a constant muse and patient editor, never ceasing to encourage me to prevail.

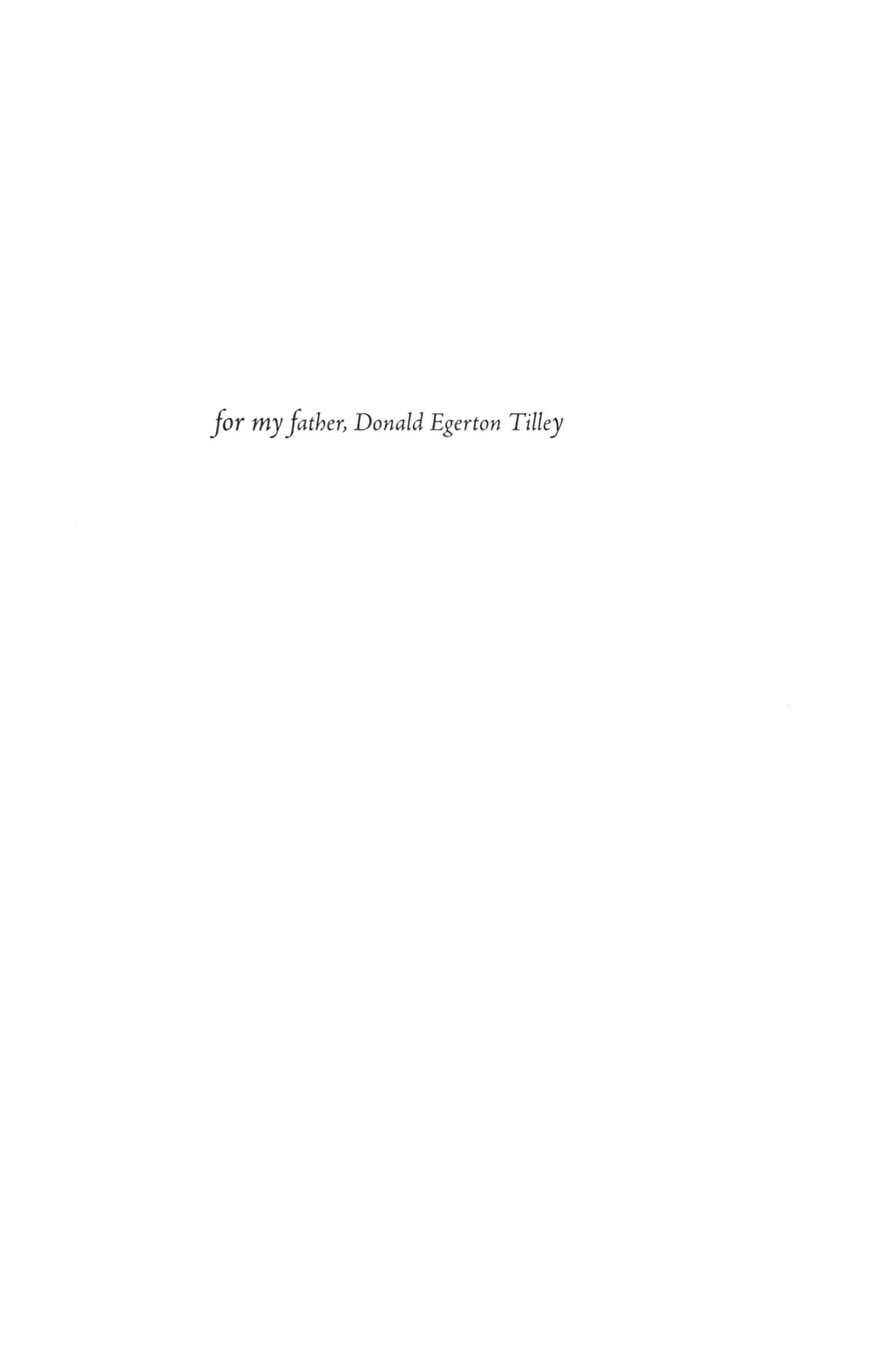

for my father, Donald Egerton Tilley

Contents

I

II

III

IV

V

This hour I tell things in confidence,
I might not tell everybody, but I will tell you.

—Walt Whitman

In Confidence

I

Murmur

Every fall and spring, we drove
to Boston to let the doctors

poke and listen, jelly our chests
for electrocardiograms.

We always stayed at the same hotel,
swam laps in the indoor pool

the night before the tests,
my son's brazen show of force

to warn whichever god was watching
that his valve worked well,

the time for carving far away.
He'd float on his back listening

for the telltale echo, backwash
against a background wash of waves,

and ask if I could hear it too.
Then he'd want to race—

one final churning length
to end this leg of the journey—

so tired afterward he'd fall asleep
before I could say goodnight.

One spring I went to Boston
alone, and returned

with a six-inch scar
to match his. He showed me

how to clutch a pillow
when I laughed, and made me

laugh hard, warned that an elephant
like his pink and grey one

would sit on my chest
for three months, then gloated

when I had six months of the same
headaches I was certain

he'd invented just for sympathy.
And as he got his first

true migraine, we compared
our blue-and-white lightning-bolt

auras that bring on splitting pain
and the clearest vision one can imagine.

Vocabulary Test

Did Joe Gargery *compassionate* towards Pip?
        my son offered as an example of good usage.
An ugly adjectival verb, was all I could say,
        then on to even less elegance in the breakfast

list of words for that day's test on a morning
        he began with two Tylenol to kill the lingering
ache from yesterday's fall down stairs at school
        where a tennis racket lunged unseen

from an eight-foot-high shelf packed with students'
        paraphernalia and conked him squarely
on the back of a concussion-proof head,
        his pediatrician said. As he left the house

to get into my idling car, some silver, gold,
        red and blue thing, nestled in the pachysandra
by the wrought-iron chairs, snagged his attention.
        This has never happened to me, he said.

Then the boy, who adored birthdays
        more than anybody else I know (all of his
stuffed animals had two per year), snatched
        the fancy balloon with Mickey and Minnie's

message: "Gotta hand it to ya. You did it."
        It's a sign! he exclaimed. No, today, that must
be a *portent,* he giggled, as I secured his treasure
        to the handle of our front door.

Things Not Asked

Son never asked whether money was tight
that Christmas father made their presents himself
or whether it was simply a professor's
need to use his hands instead of his mind,

the old jigsaw with red wooden handle,
steel U-shaped frame, and delicate blade
that would bow and catch whenever
it wasn't directed with finesse at just the right pace

through the Norman Rockwell cover
father had snipped from *The Saturday Evening Post*
and pasted onto a sheet of plywood,
the saw's tiny teeth chewing along the lines

he'd penciled on the back. The picture
could have been anything—
son never asked his sister why she always
placed every piece face side down.

Perhaps it was an early sign she'd
inherited the professor's talent for mathematics;
perhaps she just watched everyone else
struggle to differentiate one patch of blue sky

bleached with clouds from another,
and realized there's more in the shape of things
than in the picture, the shape lasting
long after the picture fades.

The Spectacles

Well before sunrise I rise and look out
past Milton Island to the pair of isles
called The Spectacles. They help me focus,
bring on a calm, one in the other's lee
unless the wind is from the north or south.
Today, the breeze riffles the river's skin
against the flow; the purple-and-gray bank
of clouds moves westward; the windsock and flag
lie momentarily limp. That will change.
Some mornings when I sit with my father,
I see an ease wash over him, his mind
become clear. But tomorrow there will be
no yellow-orange glow and we won't see
The Spectacles. Everything will fog in.

No Two Countries

Son lying in the hammock again,
loose weave of thoughts like yesterday
and the day before, the afternoon trying
to remember summer, oaks succeeding

more than maples unable to escape
their rush to reds dusted with orange.
Is he here to view the colors, he wonders,
or to watch his father

create his maps with a palette of four colors
and paint-by-numbers rules:
no two countries permitted the same color
if they touch, no single region

allowed to enclose others, no islands
like the one out there in the river
they used to explore, no ocean, just one wave
of the mathematician's hand

and whales, swordfish, krill, kelp, algae—
gone. Good-bye real world:
his geometry must be flat, not curved and closed.
Not earth, not moon.

Good-bye Sea of Tranquility. Why prove
a famous theorem already proved? son asks.
To prove it a different way, more elegantly,
father answers. To validate a life,

son thinks, father's legacy committed
to paper, time stamped, name stamped.
Einstein did this: *I* did that.
Shakespeare wrote this: *I* wrote that.

Father takes no note of his namesake
tree by the river bleeding its ruddy leaves.
Good-bye spouse and family.
Along the border of sanity, he knows

there's always somewhere he can add
or subtract a country, the mathematician
become Van Gogh, mind confined,
coloring to extinction while coloring

to stay alive. Son's hammock rocks
like a cradle, his view now smeared
with autumn's rust. White oak refuses to turn.
Bradford pear clings to summer.

Half-Finished Bridge

No important work to do today, I think,
as I lie in the hammock one last time
before storing it for winter,
just a few chores around the yard—
deck chairs to be stacked and stashed away
and the lawn raked despite the pears
and oaks hanging on to their green.

Stamped on the pencil I'm using,
first snow falling on the half-finished bridge,
now as in Bashō's time,
the halfway done possibly a road
to nowhere, like the wars we shouldn't start
and the marriages we can't finish.
But he must've meant that I find myself

amidst the season's first flurries,
leaves collecting at my feet
as I rock in the wind, writing to my father
that I'm grateful he's still alive
and there's time to erect the rest of the trestle
and walk together to the other side,
light snow falling on our backs.

Until First Snow

For you it was always gardening, the clumps
of moistened earth, the trowel's handle worn
against your palm as the seasons' annuals
found their usual spots, and while you dug,
I racked up the balls, practiced straight shots,
then banks and combinations. Just plain stuff,
no need for the fancy massé around here
where one wins by playing against oneself.
This much you knew. Now the cushions are soft,
the slate has warped, and not much rolls true
since you've been gone. I've set aside
the cue stick and let the trowel get used to me.
This summer I kept the beds free of weeds.
Fall was warm—the mums stayed until first snow.

Binoculars

I set aside the paper with its front-page notice
about Updike's death
and saw my son staring out the window
past the fence to where a large bird
pecked at the ground, beak flecked with red and sticky

bits of fur. On the ground a dead rabbit,
what else could it have been?
Then another bird, the first still picking
at the carcass, the second standing still,
wings spread full, marking the spot for others,

waiting its turn. Wild turkeys, he said,
but as I looked through the binoculars,
I could see the markings weren't right—
they were vultures and their fare
a six-point buck on its side in the snow,

an eye gouged out, a rib snapped in half
as if from a blow, right hind leg
gnawed to the bone. Then three birds,
one eating, two waiting, each knowing
its place. Okay, this is a good place

to admit I couldn't find the binoculars.
While the bird was busy feasting,
I had walked out to the fence
to perform the autopsy, and while I was
curious about the decorum in the queue,

it was the bright red blood
pooled between the bare ribs that gripped me—
how the color of life
can still inhabit the non-living,
a relationship show signs of life

though its ribs are broken
and its unseen eye no longer glistens.
Always the lingering question
about the cause of death and its precise time,
the disembodied sense of staring at oneself

and not recognizing the creature.
How you can't know when you're actually dead,
though you must have felt it.
And that is where it always expires—
the metaphor out there in the snow.

You turn away and walk back to the house
of your life, up to where
someone still stands at the window. And whatever
happened out there, you'll say you were
both right: they were turkey vultures.

From the Forest Comes the Call

—for Lennart, 12/25/2009

He'd called upon the owl one too many times,
so the turkey vulture flew down to serve
as keeper of the forest, diviner of fortune,
haruspex standing watch over a buck's
spilled entrails, patch of snow gathered at its feet
melting into augury of spring, a spring
with no guts left to tell what comes.
Before the snow was gone, coyote and crows
had finished the feast, licked ribs clean,
but not before winter's vulture saw
spring's biopsied blossoms blooming pink,
saw white blossoms bleed, leukocytes
multiply then fall away like petals.
Saw ischemia, saw the scoliotic weeping tree
bend to its arthritis, saw vitreous humor
detach from sky, saw clouds no longer hiding
from the MRIs, saw C. difficile, saw son,
wife, brother, sister, mother, father,
son's father-in-law all falling from the plum.
Now the owl is back. They say she can see
things we can't, but from the forest
comes the call, Who? Who?, and he knows
that she can't see any more than he who's next.

Chemotherapy

From the window she can see the breeze
riffle the forsythia's yellow spray,
and near the willow, her favorite magnolia,
a pointillistic pink-and-white pastel
not yet painted over by leaves.

Sometime between the wind taking
no note of bare branches
and the forest hiding behind its green,
her apple trees will become giant
dandelions gone to seed.

In this fragile equilibrium, an ether
between too many and too few,
she lies down beside her sleeping lover
to stroke his back, and almost forgets
about this time next year.

Empty Casings

The empty shell casings
are not worth anything to us.
—Lt. Gary Gallinot,
spokesperson, Santa Monica PD

My friend looked surprised when I gave him
a Cambodian peace bell for Hanukkah
and told him what it was, tiny copper chime
that villagers make for their oxen
by melting down exploded landmines,
striving to transmute their heritage of swords.

I hadn't seen him in over a year, not since
his son's bar mitzvah. I'm not a Jew,
haven't heard the story again and again
of so much light from so little oil.
Didn't grow up learning how many olives
one has to press, unlike the children

of the Bais Chabad synagogue in Santa Monica
making menorahs from the empty casings
of their PD's target practice. My friend
will soon learn more than he wants to know
about target practice, about rearing a child
as spent bullets collect on both sides,

mother unable to wean herself from the son,
father retreating into work and travel.
He will learn about the landmines in divorce,

will see how much light can come
        from the last oil of a marriage.
How hard he's finding it to press the olives,

        how hard to reclaim his heritage, his mother's
fine china passed down from her mother
        and the family brass-and-copper menorah
made by German POWs in an Allied camp
        where his father had kept them hard at work
melting down the empty casings of a war.

Private Tour

—for Slavka

Had it not been the first stop my wife and I
made that day, we might have looked for meaning
in the calf-skin-covered illuminated manuscripts
in the Strahov Monastery's libraries,
facts, but not illumination, flowing easily from our guide
in her Czech-accented English.

We visited famous synagogues and cemeteries
with headstones seated like crooked teeth,
only symbols marking the nameless graves,
and Kafka's birthplace, ordinary street corner
on the way to the main cathedraled square
in the City of a Hundred Spires.

At lunch in a curbside café, we heard about the old
Soviet regime, how her father,
an army officer, refused to join the Party,
made the difficult more difficult still,
getting her admitted into the national academy of music
like swimming the Vltava upstream.

We followed it downstream, stopping in the afternoon
for tea. My wife asked about her children,
imagining a grown daughter who'd become
a pianist and a son who'd grumbled about
learning Russian but joined the army anyway.
Our guide said there were none

and told us about her holiday long ago in Slovenia
          with her Croatian lover,
where one night she awoke to sharp abdominal pain,
          and though the surgeon could stanch
the ectopic pregnancy's hemorrhage,
          he could not save the tube. The lover left.

Over dinner, she talked about her husband.
          She ordered the fillets of fresh carp, her favorite
and his too, she said. It came with a sauce
          thinner than the one she prepares, mixing mustard
with mayonnaise and blending in herbs.
          He was not home to enjoy it last Christmas,

still in the hospital recovering from back surgery.
          She visited every evening after work,
read aloud his favorite books until he fell asleep.
          On New Year's Eve she arrived with champagne
in time to see a young nurse kiss him on the cheek,
          a kiss that grew into a child.

State of the Union

You might have thought they were talking
about how to fix the broken economy
after the bubble burst, years of squawking
about who's really the enemy,
Party A and Party B in full dispute
about the need for intervention,
her monetary policy the root
of their issues and she with no intention
of getting it under control, a grim
situation with no sign of what could
lead to recovery and no idea who
would help to set things straight, just a dim
recollection by each of having once stood
face to face solemnly saying "I do."

II

In Spring, Mathematics Are Yellow

I'm sure there's something fractal
in forsythia, not so much its chaotic sprays,
which are probably not parabolic curves
(and certainly not catenaries
hanging under the weight of blossoms),

but the contours of the bush, branch and flower
that are shaped like a year in my life
or its day or hour. Up close, I can see
each bloom has four petals, thus proving
the limits of Fibonacci's reach,

his long arm able to paint five
on the pansies I potted for my wife, but not
across the street where our neighbor buried
perennial memories of his wife ten years ago.
How odd never to have seen the daffodils

as hexagrams before. They die too soon,
unlike the dandelions that dot my yard—
too many to fight, yet finite, unlikely Fibonacci,
though undoubtedly fractal (or so Mandelbrot
would claim), always inappropriate

for bouquets of reconciliation, firmly rooted
in the life of my lawn, while the lawn of my life
goes to seed faster than an exponential plot,
and all the quantized fluff
tunnels into next year's plans, like it or not.

Mathematician's Play

—based on the well-known problem to show
that in any group of six people, there are either
(a) at least three who are perfect strangers, or
(b) at least three who know each other

(He returns with two drinks, hands one to She.)

He: Hey, can you find a triangle among the six of us?
She: Do they all have to know?
He: Well, show me three who do or three who don't.
She: You mean if they know one another?
He: Yes, but don't think of them as people.
She: I don't get your point.
He: That's it. You need to think of us as points.
She: Fine. We're all points, okay? Now what?
He: Connect all pairs by green or red lines.
She: For who's compatible and who's not?
He: Sort of, green if they know each other or else red.
She: I guess it depends what you mean by "know."
He: Well, if they never met before tonight . . .
She: Then they don't know each other.
He: Right. Remember that monochrome's the key.
She: To a pretty woman in a sleek red dress?
He: Talking to a good-looking guy with a martini.
She: So, how do you get to know a perfect stranger?

Logic

You are driven by logic: you can't think
if you're clean-shaven, but you must shave
if you want sex tonight, so you will lie

in the hammock alone for now and shave later.
Maples make good posts to hook the ends
of hammocks to, but they release pollen.

That's not good for breathing, little kindness
or much else coming without breathing,
and thus seldom in spring. Still, it's spring

and you're content because you've figured out
the shape of things, like the meaning
of that high, fiery arc of the contrail's ice

backlit by a sun already set—
fellow travelers from point A to point B
looking down on rounded, greening hills

drenched in shadow, who, given a chance,
might be inclined to show a little kindness,
but each is rushing somewhere beyond B,

only the lucky heading home to lie alone
without a worry about having to shave.
True for the women at least, if not the men.

The Big Questions

The big questions are big only
because they have never been answered.
Some questions, big as they seem,
are big only in the moment,
like when you're hiking a trail alone

and you encounter a mammoth
grizzly who hasn't had lunch
in a fortnight, and he eyes you
as the answer to his only big question.
Life turns existential, and you can't

help questioning why you are here—
in this place on this planet
within this universe—
at this precise time,
or why he is, and you know he's not,

even for a moment, wondering
the same thing, because he's already
figured it out. And you, too,
know exactly what to do.
So, this can be a defining moment,

but not a big question,
because no one ever figures those out.
Still, one day when someone does,
might it not be a person like you
staring down a bear looking for lunch?

Chamomile

I can usually count on some Chamomile
to loosen up the left brain, but today
Is Darjeeling a higher form of tea?
is enmeshed in a network of neurons
looking for answers to *Do gods evolve?*
And then the unsolicited cascade—
Can anything evolve without learning?
Do gods have anything to learn? Aren't gods
our creations? If we evolve, don't they?
Why so many gods? Who is the greatest?
Why must we always fight over our gods?
But with characteristic good manners,
patiently waiting its turn, the right brain
answers: *Because they won't fight over us.*

Grand Design

No reason to worry whether the cotton
arms of a galaxy will work
Leo was thinking. Ear dust
not stardust when he saw his wife

wrap a cotton ball
around the end of a toothpick
and stick it in Baby Gerstenzang's ear.
No thoughts of index finger

and opposing thumb, no engineer's feat
to make an elbow or wrist
all over again when the only goal
is cleaning an ear. No need for

a grand unified theory of anything.
Getting cotton to adhere to wood
that wouldn't splinter
was Leo's problem, his part to play,

and it took years, not days,
Leo so hard at work he had no time
to marvel at a dawn's cotton gaze
or watch shadows begin to slink

beneath a fieldrow of cotton stalks
as woodland hills burst into light,
another morning sparked into being.
When he earned his day of rest,

who says Leo didn't find himself
lost in clouds, the grand design forgot?
Maybe like a god, he wondered why
he made the thing he made.

Plywood Palace

it was called thirty years ago after window panes
began to fall. From his office, he watched one
break apart on the sidewalk, young actuary
figuring the probabilities of loss.

The first an accident, the second a coincidence,
the third a pattern: plywood replacing glass
soon gave the building a checkerboard face,
eyesore that had to be painted black.

Double-panes the problem, Engineers & Architects
concluded, single sheets of mirrored glass the answer,
and Bostonians joked
about the power of the setting sun

reflected from the tower's western face
setting Newton's famous elms ablaze.
Of course that never happened, but the edifice
gave rise to lawsuits as it sank

into Back Bay's landfill, cracking the foundation
of a hotel and entire transept of Trinity Church.
And cartoons, one in the *Tech*,
MIT's student newspaper: perplexed man staring

at an elevator panel with all floor numbers
Xed out and marked one less. Of course the ground floor
never became the basement,
and everything's settled now, but the building,

thin as a foil, still roils the air, collects
small breezes, turns them into winds on Copley Square,
near-gales that once popped windows out
and whipped up blizzards of glass

scoring everything in their path
down Clarendon Street. Now, only the butterfly effect—
chaos exported everywhere—
which, way back then, not even actuaries could see.

Richter 7.8

Dark energy and dark matter describe proposed solutions to as yet unresolved gravitational phenomena. So far as we know, the two are distinct.

—Robert Caldwell, cosmologist,
SciAm.com, August 28, 2006

Such a waste to spend a life thinking
about the impossible to figure out, like where the spirit
goes when detached from its body.

An alternate universe perhaps. That's where
dark matter enters, not how physicists hypothesize,
but the way it casts light on everyday affairs.

I, for one, am stuck on the question
of how dark matter and energy can be separate and distinct
when plain mass and energy are equivalent.

We're told we need both types of darkness
to fill what's missing, yet one pulls us together
while the other propels us apart.

What we can't find in our world must be
the substance of another,
worlds that look to each other for what's missing,

each a resting place for the other's souls,
an answer to why any god would allow a quake
to bury nine hundred children under a school,

what's so incomprehensible here on earth
maybe making sense in the place where all those students
have found new flesh to wear.

Serendipity in the Cosmos

I could try to deal with the big question
of why any of us is present in this universe,
but that would cause me to set aside
the immediate matter of why I was absent

from my bedroom yesterday afternoon,
not reclining against the pillows as I
usually am, reading poetry before I succumb
to the warmth of the late-day sun.

It would also force me to shelve the questions
of why my son took up golf at age four,
why we bought this Tudor house
fourteen years ago, with a lawn barely

large enough for a full wedge shot, yet far too
vast to maintain ourselves, and how we found
our immigrant gardener of ten years,
whose men forever struggle against the tug

of their mowing machines with spinning blades
that occasionally catch a stray stone
embedded in the rough and sling it as if towards
some unknown enemy who does not realize

his fortune is about to change. It is no small thing
that the workers came this week on Monday
when Tuesday is their usual day,
and in the afternoon instead of morning,

and I have to wonder why, after all the years
his mother told him not to play in the backyard,
my son grabbed a fistful of old Titleist balls
last fall before he returned to college,

still not listening at age twenty-one,
and knocked them back and forth across the lot,
then left them strewn upon the lawn
for a workman to snag as he tilted and turned

the lumbering hulk of his mower. It remains
a mystery how the dimpled projectile managed
to arc its way into the third-story bedroom,
leaving a telltale hole in the pane

of a window normally swung wide open
to let in fresh air, but cranked shut after the April
heat wave broke. Of course, you say,
it is now clear why there was little resistance,

the inside winter storm having been removed,
the summer screen raised, the indoor
shutters not drawn because the sun was not yet
low enough to be blinding, but no one,

not even the muses, can explain why
my ex-wife decided yesterday that it was time
at last to cast off her heavy blanket of loneliness
and have me take some smiling photographs

to post to her friends, thus causing me
to edit her favorite few on the laptop computer
in my office far away from the spray of leaded glass
that showered the spot still cooling

on my pillow where I had left the May issue
of *Poetry* opened up to Jane Hirshfield's
"Assay Only Glimpsable for an Instant," one moment
black and white and then a rainbow of color.

Fish Story

I couldn't see anything in the eyes
of the spiny brown-and-white striped
blowfish swept far up onto the beach
and left stranded on wet sand sweating
in the sun. I set down my camera,
and peered past the gold rims,

through the lenses and deep into the
dark, primordial wells of the fish,
and it looked back into the same spot
in my being. There we touched,
inner fish to inner fish. In my best
silent fishspeak, I told it there was

a parable, even a higher purpose—
that it had been chosen to show us
things don't always work out,
that one can't always penetrate the foam
or fathom that bubbles in the churn
can suddenly become gaping holes

in the universe's vast underbelly of hope.
Then I stopped, because I could tell
it hadn't understood, or no longer
cared. I could see it felt no empathy
for the rest of us swaddled in froth.
Besides, its spines looked poisonous.

The Breakers

No clouds that morning, but things were out there
waiting to be photographed. Using his new camera,
the hotel guest caught a surfer tumbling headlong,
the red wetsuit not much more than a dot on the seam
between light-blue sky and dark-blue ocean.
He snapped a gray-backed ring-billed gull
on the breakwall, half-coming, half-going, the picture
splitting two birds, making them appear the halves
of a disjointed whole, like *he* often found himself,
right-and-left-brained and cortical-and-limbic
at the same time. He saw the strong surge sweep
a brown-and-white striped blowfish far up onto
the sand, leaving it swaddled in froth, and he knelt
to get a closer look at the gold-rimmed eyes,
glowing rings around wells of blackness neither he
nor his camera could fathom. He waited for the next
wave, but it came up short and retreated quickly.
The tide was turning, and there would be no help
for the creature, unless another person happened by
who didn't mind the slimy skin or prickly spines,
someone like his ex-wife, the other half, with whom
he once walked that beach on a cloudless day.

III

Message

A part of you wants to cast off the extraneous,
make life into haiku, and keep the other part in tow
before the ink runs dry, the metaphor told to stay tidy,
even though the message is in the mess
and age. But it's seldom the word you go looking for;
it's the words you find.

Why is the world? you asked, and ran to *World Books*
as if someone who came before you
had the answers and written them down,
as if in reading them, you'd find better questions
to ask of the glossy color pictures that defined
the end of childhood, as if in knowing,

you could push time forward, figure out how 2050
turns out, transform the world into a giant equation
with a supercomputer powerful enough to solve it,
then watch the map above the homeroom blackboard
morph before your eyes, see Yugoslavia
finish its splintering and the U.S.S.R. lose its U,

rain forests disappear with the rain, Greenland turn green,
honey bees die off. And look backward, too—
sit at the honey-colored desk in history class
beside the girl who kept showing you
her panties the year she made you
miss the lesson of Rhodesia beginning to grow

into what would become Zimbabwe's skin,
when what you could do at the World's Fair
without your parents mattered more
than the world going round and round
and up and down, before the Olympics mattered more
than world fairs, long before

you bought your own honey-colored desk,
where you made your son write
I will not strike my brother lines in ballpoint pen,
the antique grade school desk with a hole for bottles
of India ink you'd get all over your fingers
when you tried to refill your fountain pen

from the well, and afterwards, soap and water
merely lightened the stains. Back to first grade
before you cared what was under a girl's underpants,
back when you were made to write lines over and over,
no one yet in your life to write love notes to,
long before the mess that age and love can bring.

India Ink

You hauled it down from the attic for your grandson,
the honey-colored desk where you
once made me write *I will not strike my brother*
lines in ballpoint pen, like the antique

grade school desk with a well for bottles of ink
only India seemed to make
that I'd get all over my fingers and thumbs
when I fumbled with filling

my fountain pen, and afterwards, soap and water
merely lightened the stains.
First grade, my name in cursive, my name in cursive,
over and over on wide-ruled sheets

the teacher marked as if it were a punishment
my striving for an exquisite signature
that might end up on famous accords. Now my son,
maybe President some day, signing

landmark treaties on human rights, global warming
and free trade, at last an agreement
on multi-lateral nuclear disarmament.
Ornate fountain pens, hands never quite clean.

In Confidence

Why does leaning on the rail of a deck
and looking out over layers of hills
as buds burst through their coverings
evoke the big questions? Like why
are we making such a mess of it all?

Ask Sunday's dissonant choir of birds
in the newspaper's Week in Review,
always a replay of the same
failures. Lots of cartoons there
to remind us that making fun of ourselves

is a start but not an end. Take today—
though it could be any day—
a young girl with a bow in her hair
asking her bald-headed ex-VP granddad
to teach her new dog a trick,

so he grasps the pup by its scruff,
and pours a glass of water down its throat
while screaming, Speak! Speak!
I know we should, but it's so hard
to feel tortured out here

watching the oak unfold its leaves.
Besides, waterboarding sounds like
an amusement park ride,
what you might do with your kids
at Typhoon Lagoon. I know I would

give up secrets. That's why
you should never trust me with one,
though I must admit
that your brief affair with a colleague
will always be safe with me.

After Wine

I thought of the Middle East
as I washed the lone
whole wine glass

after sweeping up
a thousand fragments,
one shard long and jagged

like the boundary
demarcation on a map
where a sacred river

divides a people,
and many tiny crystals
no longer dancing

as they did the night before
in the lancing light
of the near-full moon

that must also have burst
into bedrooms over there
where others were making love.

Folding

I stare blankly at my mother-in-law's longhand
legacy to her daughter, Crisco thumbprints smearing
some of the India ink. My wife's away and my son

waits for his Sunday pancakes as I puzzle over
Fold buttermilk and an egg into the dry ingredients.
No hints, merely a warning. I've learned

that major perils attend misfolding, that proteins
stuck mid-stream, half-folded on the way
to proper states, can transform a normal brain

into bubbly batter with lumps. I've been taught
how to fold laundered shirts and sheets,
items I burn at times while ironing out problems,

but never as badly as the toast I charred today.
I unfold the morning paper, sit down with my black
coffee to digest the Week in Review, and note

as I read about the latest bombings that recipes
don't always turn out right, that sometimes
it may be better to fold, even for the Master Chef.

Dislocation

It's like there's a magnet lodged in my brain,
drawing current through the same synapses
when I try to write. Electric shrapnel—
words and body parts pasted together
by Picasso. I find myself making
raw anagrams of *war,* a *suicide*
bomber scattering *bard typos* in his
own *tablet* against the enemy, here
an *ebb curse idiom,* there a *busied*
microbe. Hard enough to *bide orb miscues*
every day, but why sacrifice ourselves
to *imbed bio curses,* like the one
that's wormed deep into my frontal cortex
and spoiled the poem I had wanted to write?

Boys

My friends and I couldn't buy cherry bombs
on our weekly allowances. We hoped
that plain firecrackers would be enough
to tear off arms and legs, a private's, not ours.
We were the generals—we ran the war,
decided where to plant soldiers in trenches
we sculpted in mounds left by bulldozers
on the construction site. After the flap
about the Curry boy losing an eye,
we imposed a ceasefire for a week.
Then came the all-out surge to do some
serious damage, the kind that requires you
to eat two bowls of cornflakes every day
to build your army from cereal-box toys.

One Would Hope

that life's final moments travel slowly,
quieting the blood and brain and leaving
time enough to hear one's choice of music,
a plucked lute for the teenage boy driving
through a crowded street—barely entering
a Baghdad square to gather his father
from work, talking to his mother about
new friends at school or scoring the winning
goal in a soccer game—when the bursts
of bullets rang. And for the mother
leaning on her son, a lullaby, the one
her mother sang to her, and she to him.
For both of them, one would hope that life
was long enough to hear each other's song.

The Ivy and the Brick

As usual, it was nothing of great consequence
that made me stop. This time, ivy grown thick
between columns of windows on a brick building
that looked a few hundred years old.

It wasn't the sweat starting to collect at my temples
and throat, only eight in the morning,
no breeze yet and the hazy air refusing
to succumb to the sun. It wasn't the weight

of the golf bag slung over my shoulder
as I walked up the path to where my son
would tee off for a tournament. Just the ivy and brick,
how little time it takes for ivy

to fill an empty space, how often it must be pruned
to keep windows clear, and how long
it must have taken to learn how to make brick.
How necessary the clay and the fire,

and the manual labor before machines.
How hard we work to build and maintain,
how easily we tear things down; how hard
it would be to wake to a world blown away,

how much easier to play a round of golf,
even if it had to be with a hickory shaft
and rusted iron for a club and boiled goose feathers
covered with bull's hide for a ball.

The Clay and the Fire

I see diggers winning clay with hand shovels,
preparers working and pugging it,

clot molders shaping rough lumps, brick molders
dashing those into beechwood casts,

trimming the excess with strikes, then stackers
stacking bricks herringbone in the sun,

edgers with their clappers, stackers again, stacking
in a hackstead covered with straw.

I see fire in scove kilns, low heat for two days,
bricks yielding their watersmoke,

intense heat for a week, fireholes bricked over
for another week, the sorting,

clinkers going to garden paths, the perfectly fired
to the exteriors of buildings.

And here I walk along a clay path
toward a brick library to return this book

on the art of making bricks, wondering how long
it would take to rediscover the art—

if we could, if we would even want to—
that is, if we lost all our tools and books,

if had we reduced everything to rubble,
if we could actually do that to ourselves.

Every Branch

According to the November 6, 2008 issue
of the *Harvard Gazette* (page 2), the Corporation
closed the Veterinary School in 1900,
no prejudice against pets, just a matter of finance,

the endowment not full enough
for doctors of animals, likely a small squeeze
requiring choices, not like this
global meltdown, the giant flywheel of selling

long past its moment of inertia,
no more stoppable now than the drying out
of peat bogs in the northern latitudes,
the unrelenting letting loose of CO_2 (pages 5 & 8),

certainly not the essence of joy,
the essence of a Yeats poem
Professor Vendler laid bare (pages 5 & 6).
No longer does it matter whether they cease

producing the *Gazette* in print.
No one can save the forest
that fueled the fires that burned down
the houses of derivatives; if only it had been

winter when Harvard graduates (or was it MIT?)
concocted those creations. They could have
peered into the woods and seen
the naked souls of branches branching,

a network of everything connecting everything;
they could have figured out
that when a tree falls—whether we hear it or not—
so does every end of every branch.

Loss of Purchase

It has come from the cedar-shake roof
heading downward onto the bedroom window,
hind claws clutching a muntin, fore claws
screeching on the pane, glistening eyes

motionless, fully stretched body unable
to secure a purchase, unable to turn around
and climb back up, unable to continue
toward the ground, unable to leap ten feet

sideways to the pergola's slats—stuck—
white belly flat against the glass,
common gray squirrel like an investor
caught between a bad buy and a worse sell

with no choice but freefall and thud
on the wooden deck below, lifeless for minutes
until a top-to-bottom tremor as it vacates
bladder and bowels, nervous system

in hard reboot, front paws holding the head,
rear legs planted in the spreading pool,
body listing to the right, and finally the eyes
blinking back on before it scampers away,

not quite restored, not quite knowing
what has just occurred, soon to be bored again
with ordinary trees and ready to find the roof,
unlikely to remember the fall.

Running Free

It's a yacht race, for God's sake, said the owner
of the syndicate that won the last two
America's Cups, Mr. Bertarelli,
of his suit to prevent Mr. Ellison,
another billionaire, from competing
in the next event with his syndicate's
newly launched trimaran. It's about
how we put our money into wind, you think,
as you stand knee-deep in Nantucket Sound
watching a kite surfer take some air
and turn about. How we utilize
the molecules of air beyond mere breathing,
like that hovering tern, who, unlike you,
doesn't know the Bernoulli equation.

The tern adjusting its wings, the tern who
doesn't employ designers and engineers
to build the best bird, but on biofuel
alone is more efficient than any plane.
The tern who doesn't care that Professor Betz
proved that a mere sixteen twenty-sevenths
is the highest fraction of energy
we can convert from wind, whether sailboat,
bird or turbine—it flies anyway.
It's about how close we get, about trying,
like the Isle of Eigg's residents, Scots
who make do with sun, wind and waterfall.
It's all they've got and all they need, so they
fill their sails and forget the rest of us.

Out there on the Sound, you can let the sun
beat on your face, take the helm and watch
the spinnaker fill out, let yourself run free
and forget the physics professor
who kept you inside one sunny, windy day
to prove that the energy in a wave
is proportional to its amplitude squared,
when what you wanted instead was to trim
a sail and skim along the waves, take some air
and turn about or jibe beneath the terns,
a day so clear you could almost see straight
to Nantucket, but of course you couldn't,
no more than you could imagine a wind farm
out there and wind no longer merely wind.

Vase of Tall White Stalks

His friends and family know his tendencies—
today, he's at home again
knee-deep in thought,
feet anchored in Nantucket Sound

where a kite surfer catches some air
and turns about. Farther out,
a sailboat runs free. A tern
adjusts its wings to hover overhead.

Here the wind is everywhere,
and everywhere, the need is now.
It's in his face most days,
the specter of whirring metal towers out there,

the Sound become a vase
of tall white stalks he helped create
the need for—
egg beaters for the fog

that terns will learn to dodge,
a stand of beacons blinking into night,
crying out to gods and aliens,
We're here to stay until the sun burns out!

Wading further in, up to his neck,
then over his head
and bobbing in the waves,
he recalls when wind was merely wind.

Something to Celebrate

Leashless, we followed our hounds along the shore,
often stooping to search among the shells
for an explanation of the day-old news
from a country still in the mood for hanging.
Easy to say it was the full moon.
Over there, killing-time. And here we were,
killing time while our friend dug for oysters
to go with champagne for the new year,
thankful that some things hang by as little
as a thread, like the front line of seaweed
marking high tide, polar ice caps melting
slowly enough for now. But it was too cold
for thinking. We cinched our scarves and turned back,
dogs in tow. The high clouds meant first snow.

IV

On the Art of Patience

With a Mozart concerto in the background
and little to do as I waited for the next available associate
to be with me shortly, I began to comprehend
how one infinity can be larger than another,
not in the sense of the mathematician
who can prove that rational numbers are countable
and real numbers are not, but my patience,
which I am continually thanked for,
the next available associate undoubtedly

unaware of my infinite fascination with Mona Lisa's
excised eye staring upside down
from the minute hand, obliterating the smile at half past
the hour on the artisanal timepiece
my wife brought back from Florence last year.
A larger infinity is what my neighbor's cow
exhibits every day lying near the split-rail fence,
alone with her thoughts as the cars whoosh by.
This morning, she half sat, watching the sky clear

after a gauzy, misting rain that Constable
would have captured in a pastoral scene,
though the cars would have been horses,
and they would likely have been grazing when the sun
broke through and beat on their backs, the life
of horses not so different from the life of cows
or people on hold, or even an artist like Reinhardt
whose work seemed to be rushed near the end
of his life, no doubt the reason

he turned to monochromes and they turned so black,
        the tall rectangles of earlier paintings
ceding their space to smaller squares, the subtle changes
        in hue and tone maybe discernible by others,
but not me, though they might have been
        had I been able to view one at MoMA
under different light and catch a trace
        of the mountains at deep dusk he must first have
brushed onto the canvas, followed by a beach

        with bathers clad only in dark skin, then a black
haystack with Black-Eyed Susans off to the right,
        and ending with a self-portrait that explicated
his choice of color—undetailed, unremitting, permitting,
        no not permitting, but coercing
the viewer's mind to co-exist with the artist's, as in
        stepping into Gaudí's forest of columns
that draw one's eyes to a ceiling where porphyritic trunks
        branch into geometry, the redwood canopy

leaving no sense of outside world, there being no sign
        of anyone's god lurking in the stained glass,
no resolution of apse from transept amidst a thicket
        of rusted iron shafts and crossbeams,
scaffold for the project he couldn't complete in a lifetime,
        that may never be finished in anyone's lifetime
my wife and I concluded as we passed through
        the timelessness of the cathedral on our recent trip
to Barcelona. Finishing is not the point in art,

just calling it quits when one runs out of patience
or some other project commandeers the mind,
which brings to mind the plight of the pandas,
a species also on hold, who, like their forebear
Ling Ling, have trouble procreating
in captivity, the problem not that there aren't enough
bamboo shoots or Eucalyptus leaves
to keep them healthy and amorous, or enough open space
to tango with a mate,

but unlike the cow trying to insinuate herself
into the Constable landscape, the female panda
doesn't see the point of lying around
feigning lack of interest until her consort
springs into action. Or perhaps she can see
the thing is being filmed and refuses to take part
in panda porn, isn't fooled or moved by Mozart
saturating the air from speakers hidden in trees,
no more than I was for 19 minutes and 57 seconds

(no, Mona Lisa doesn't have a second hand,
but the rose-gold Tourneau that my wife
bought me in New York City does)
kindly continuing to hold for the next available associate
at William Ashley, sole Canadian distributor
for the English Portmeirion Botanic Garden collection
of fine china, in particular the six 8"-diameter
pasta bowls featuring the Treasure Flower,
Eastern Hyacinth, Sweet William, Garden Lilac,

Dog Rose, and Belladonna Lily, their common names.
          Later, with more time, though for no good reason,
I was able to find the Latin appellations,
          which, in the interest of space, I won't provide.
Did I mention that I was trying to buy the pasta bowls
          for my mother's 80th birthday in two weeks' time?
Or that the next available associate told me
          they were out of stock? Would you like
the salad bowls instead? she asked.

A Belated Calculus

Like an old retiree, Goldstein's been shelved,
collecting dust, exactly as he was throughout
that college course some thirty years ago—
the ABCs of *Classical Mechanics*

instructed by the dour Dr. Stevenson
who couldn't instill in students any affection
for the alphabet of physics. Well, Professor,
I've learned to set your *apsides* aside

for astronomers revolving in their own
eccentric orbits, and *brachistochrones*
for builders of fortunes riding the stock market
roller coaster. But *catenaries* strangle

a little of the aesthete in me every day
that my town's telephone poles stand askew,
their high-strung wires pleasing only birds,
who line up like abacus beads,

moving into place, I suppose, by the same
unseen physical force that draws me
somewhat further down the row of textbooks
to my son's high school poetry reader

with its tattered jacket and yellowing leaves.
Today, it opens up right to Updike
and his "Telephone Poles," as ever *more constant*
than evergreens by being never green.

Slaying Philistines

When we are no longer children,
we are already dead.
— Constantin Brancusi

Perhaps it's a story of happenstance
that begins with a village carpenter
and ends with a master in his dusty atelier,

always the unschooled shepherd
who harbors no ambitions
to lead an army, but dreams
of a magical bird, the mythical Maiastra
lifting him to perch with her
on a boulder at the edge of space
where they'll cajole a falcon's wings to stillness
and wax them with the sun,

or perhaps it's about a boy's hunger
to mold a piece of goat cheese,
whittle branches into wands, massage shavings
between his thumb and fingers, rub toes
against a stream's smooth stones,

for how else can you explain
an old man hunched over
a rhombic block of marble, carving
plainsong into crescendo, chiseling away
the husk, struggling
to liberate a creature's spirit?

Fish at the Dance

You've walked from the gallery
where a bird in space
materialized in the mind
of a peasant boy tending sheep,
featureless bronze buffed to high luster
carved into one long sweeping curve
whose equation he could not fathom,
and now you're swimming the depths
of his ocean, staring at blue-gray
mottled marble—
no tail, no fins, no scales,
no gills, no eyes—
headed for the stairway
where against the landing's wall
five salmon-skinned women
join hand-in-hand in dance,
Matisse's circle not quite closed,
still a spot for Brancusi's creature
making the leap.

Rehearsal

Leaning back in her flamingo-pink crocheted hat
not pulled quite snug, lime green plugs

showing in her ears, glasses tipped a bit
at the end of her nose, her velvet burgundy sleeve

drawn neatly to the elbow to free her wrist,
with each stroke the old woman coaxes the notes

from the page, eighths, sixteenths, thirty-seconds
coming quick, her right hand gliding outward

from her chest as it parts the air, then ceasing
without seeming to, a stilling of the delicate wing,

like an osprey drafting the currents above
her treetop nest, then drawn toward it again,

another ephemeral pause, another featherlike wave
of her right hand away from her breast,

cycling faster, slower, faster, the faint white
wisps outside the window bleaching into the sky's

faded blue denim, as they almost always do
when she's wearing her jeans to play at high altitude,

husband asleep in his leather fauteuil, the four
slightly splayed fingers of her right hand arched

across the absent bow resting on the thumb below,
a ballerina's arm and fingers moving to the score,

her head cocked to the left, her eyes half closed,
each unbroken sweep of her hand lifting a phrase,

she alone in a sound-filled space until she holds
the final note, throat quivering as the piece dissolves.

The air no longer resonant, the music now folded
and put back in its envelope, clasp fastened,

sleeve eased down onto her wrist again, her hat
pulled tight about her ears, her chair snapped back

into its upright pose, glasses pushed up along her
angular nose, eyes glistening in the day's late rays,

her face awash in transient smile, the bird
at rest in her nest, her mate unmoved in his place.

Aluminum Rush

Aluminium et design, Musée des beaux-arts,
Montréal, August 23 to November 4, 2001

You kick back on a serpentine chaise
fashioned from soda-can squares,

soak up the shade of an all-season maple
with leaves that won't rust, stain or peel.

You listen to your favorite heavy metal
played on light-metal guitars

and begin to feel the awesome power
of element #13, the promise of the future.

Before you stands the motorcycle
you've always wanted to own, the essence

of light, reflecting sun that streams
onto the Musée des Beaux Arts exhibition.

You imagine hopping aboard and riding
into the heavens, passing Icarus

on his way down to another close encounter
with your high school English teacher,

through the surface of Brueghel's painting
and into the lines of Auden's poem.

You can't help but pity poor Daedalus;
if only he'd known about aluminum,

he could have saved himself a lot of wax
and spared the masters their oils and ink.

The Photographs

1.

From Errol Morris's *New York Times* blog,
we learn that the technology didn't exist
during the Civil War to print photographs
in newspapers, and we learn that no one

knows how the tavern keeper came to possess
the ambrotype of three young children
who didn't learn for nearly six months
that their father had been killed at Gettysburg,

not until their mother read in the *American
Presbyterian* a description of that photograph,
her girl and older boy dressed in clothes
made from the same material, it said,

her younger boy seated between them,
the final view their father had of his children,
eyes fixed on the photo, then suddenly still
as the battle continued. We can imagine

a movie—the sounds of cannon fire growing
fainter, the field of corpses blurring,
the soldier's hands fading away, only the
ambrotype in sharp relief. When the scene

comes back into focus, the photo's in the hands
of a civilian physician who'd been on his way
to tend the war's wounded. For reasons
not even he will likely ever fully figure out,

the doctor has persuaded the tavern keeper
to give him the picture of the children. He wants
to return it to the unknown soldier's wife,
he says, to let her know how her husband died.

2.

Il y a longtemps que je t'aime, a thought
that might have been the soldier's last,
but here it's the title of a Claudel film
in which a parole officer also has a quest,

a photograph on the wall behind his desk
showing the Orinoco River widened nearly
into a lake and reminding him every day
of his dream to travel to South America

to find the true source, an almost impossible
search in any era, the watershed so vast
it extends into the deep reaches of Venezuela
and Brazil. One can't just start at the end,

a large delta emptying into the Atlantic,
and work one's way back upstream
along every branch. But he never even tried
because it was only his dream. Somewhere

he might have realized it would be easier
to trace his lifetime back into its jungle
and figure out exactly where it was
that he'd actually started to live. He was

different from the doctor who couldn't
leave the call of the unknown alone.
And here you'll have to resist asking
what happened—he was a minor character

and the film was about something else.
Still, who could blame you for wondering?
It's often the minor players who are
most like us.

Western Culture

Before dawn and breakfast, I wander through
The Geography of Thought, responding
in a mostly Western way to the various
questions until I meet a cow and a choice
for her partner between A) Hen and B) Grass.
I know that feng shui calls for the cow
and grass together in a field, less grass
perhaps than rain-glazed rice waving in wind.
But I also feel the hen's urge to belong—
in the barnyard beside the cow, beside
the red wheelbarrow. Today, as always
for me, it comes down to a matter of taste:
A) steak and eggs or B) milk and grains?
So much depends upon geography.

The Way We Are

Humans are promiscuous
in their omnivory. We can
eat almost anything and do . . .
in prodigious quantities.
—Noreen Tuross, Harvard University,
Professor of Scientific Archaeology

She was talking about Neanderthals,
a particular Neanderthal
who lived in the Shanidar Cave
in Northern Iraq, and about his preference
for escargot—not simmered
in white wine and garlic butter and served
with slices of crusty French bread;
no, just the garden variety
scooped out of their shells with fingernails
gritty from scratching in the dirt.

You might think that Tuross
was talking about modern man, excessive
in his dining habits, and that she
intended to venture into America's tendency
to gluttony. Not so.

The symposium turned to Europeans
and how they came to be
dairy farmers, how they discovered the land
was better used for cows than crops,
the gene variant for lactase persistence

taking hold more than 7,000 years ago,
breast-fed youngsters suddenly able
to digest animal milk well into adulthood.

The symposium didn't address
prodigious promiscuous prehistoric appetites
per se, but picture this:
Old man aged forty sitting on a rock
outside his hut savoring warm milk
as he ogles every big-breasted, fat-lipped,
wide-hipped village girl who ambles by,
fantasizing about a hearty meal
with a few dozen of them down by the stream,
if not dinner tonight,
then surely breakfast tomorrow.

Smoked Tuna and Kalamata Olive Pâté

It is necessary, and fair, to let you know
before you wade in too far
that you will not find the customary melancholy or lament
because the day has offered none,
other than just three of us this year,
our friend's wife away. No picture of you
and her leaning shoulder-to-shoulder,
hair blowing in the breeze. Yet no sadness or distress,
because we've chosen not to see

the great white that might have caught
the scent of the two seals frolicking along the shore
unaware one of their kind had been lost
near here a few weeks ago. And did you notice

the gray-backed gull venturing toward lunch
was not put off by my tossing stones in its direction?
It sniffed as if they were bits of bluefish,
or pepper cracker smeared with tapenade. Remember
the smoked tuna and Kalamata olive pâté
was only ever for us.

Didn't it become clear as the weather laid down
that two bottles of chilled Magito
can always wash away the larger clouds?

Beneath the fine dry white surface to the cooler moister
coarser sand below, I dug without thinking
about what slips through fingers,

the act of grasping handfuls and letting each sift away
as hypnotic as the white noise of Monomoy's Atlantic surf,
where a few hours earlier

I'd let cold waves
break at my ankles and froth around my thighs
to carry off the poison
ivy I'd brushed against along the path
through the dune grasses from the island's inner side
where we'd left the rocking boat at anchor
in the ebbing tide.

No thoughts of quahogging the flats for dinner
as the afternoon pinked us up,
bug spray keeping the few September greenheads at bay,
everything logy under the sun
filtered by

the thin scattered clouds,
low, portending nothing, the seas at most a foot,
no cell phones or radios, no concerns
about what might happen between the lingering now
and when we'll be back next year, all four.
Just me looking at you in your one-piece black bathing suit,
thinking what one can do when there are only two.

Horrifying of Highness

The Chinese prepared for the onslaught
of English-speaking visitors, translated
their ubiquitous ideograms into signs
like: *Please don't touch yourself.*
Let us help you try out. Thank you.
Easy enough to understand, but what about

the Beijing billboard that advertises
testes to make your heart tinkle?
Who has the balls to hurt you?
You can think of plenty, but another
sign reminds you of *those who suffer*
from high blood pressure mental disease

horrifying of highness.
There's a certain arrogance in assuming
facility with another's mother tongue
and in its cousin who insists that people
speak his well or not at all.
I'm now speaking of the French—

in particular, of a certain athlete,
who assured the world his team
would "smash" the U.S. swim team,
but was then out-touched by an American
who closed an impossible gap
with less than a quarter lap to go,

leaving the French in second place,
        stunned, in a fog like some *liquor head*
the morning after a binge
        suddenly having lost the testicles it took
to get himself into a twist in the first place.
        It made your heart tinkle

while sitting on the edge of a sofa that night,
        initially horrifying of highness
and hoping for comeuppance,
        then transfixed, incredulous,
ecstatic at the precipitous fall.
        Two faces, nothing lost in translation.

Dirty Laundry

ALL WORK DONE ON PREMISE, says the yellow
sign stenciled on the side of a blue van,
intended to assure that the shirts,
trousers, skirts, blouses, dresses, socks and wraps,
even the underwear, will be laundered
or dry cleaned, as appropriate, by the people
who work at the establishment, people
you know, who will care for your clothes as you would,
if only you were so inclined, and weren't
otherwise so thoroughly engaged.
But what if the missing letter is no mistake,
the fine print rendered large, ruined when they
laundered instead of dry cleaned it, because, like you,
they have long since stopped liking what they do?

Gradients

Season of wind and rain, gale force
bursts that sweep across the reservoir

ripping leaves from autumn trees
and pasting them against the stucco,

the house shaking so hard
ceiling moldings split. From the attic's

window seat, a view for miles
of oaks bending to their breaking points.

For the ancients, it was plane trees
that made them bow before the fury

of their gods and sacrifice their goats.
We let *our* goats make milk, but burn

ourselves at the altar, find a shrink
to fix the inner cracks. Why not

climb the stairs, curl up with pillows,
and gaze out beyond the gazebo

to weeping cherry and pear? Face
a season's rage, ceding only leaves.

Variations on a Theme by Yeats

black swans on a pond
sprinkled with late autumn leaves
waiting for the freeze

~

Easy to count the black swans on the pond
sprinkled with late leaves—they seek company.
The first arrives on the surge of its bow wave;
four others pass beneath the footbridge
in pursuit. Five, not fifty-nine. Why they
can't migrate I'm not sure. I can, but don't.
Perhaps it's the seasons in a world that
seems too constant otherwise, every day
the same old news, same old wounds, the ones
hard to keep bandaged up. I haven't
figured out what I'm seeking, but I'm glad
for the company of swans. You'd think they'd
leave. They likely would if they could, instead
of waiting with me for the pond to freeze.

~

On cold, sunny days I walk the dirt road past this estate, making my nearly imperceptible bow wave in the world. I don't know what I'm seeking, but certainly not company. I prefer my own, especially now my beagle lies confined at home by hip boot and collar to keep her from pawing the foot she scratched through fur and flesh down to bone. Is that the difference? I don't have an itch for anything, yet I worry the wounds we inflict upon ourselves, the ones hard to keep bandaged up. Things I don't need to tell you who are wearied lover by lover, who already know the trees are past their autumn beauty. On this duck pond sprinkled with late leaves, red-beaked black swans among the stones, silhouettes against the water-mirrored sky. Where I stand at the edge, one arrives on the surge of its bow wave; three others pass beneath the wooden footbridge in pursuit, and one has already come and gone around the tiny island. Five, not fifty-nine. Easy to count these brilliant creatures that cannot mount and scatter, wheeling in great broken rings. Though their hearts have not grown old, they cannot leave. I don't know why. I can, but don't. Perhaps it's the seasons in a world too constant otherwise, every day the same old news. I'm glad for the company of swans, the certainty of knowing I won't wake some day to find they've flown away. Together, we wait for the pond to freeze.

Into Her World

Her nose tells her it's something, nothing
I could see on a normal day, but the wind
has gathered the light first snow into piles
among clumps of dried grass left from the late
November cutting. Unmistakable
fresh prints—deer hooves here and rabbit paws there.
Today, I left the same old road, ducked through
a split rail fence, willing to share my beagle's
anticipation. Now I let her tug
the leash, drag me across a field into
brambles at the edge of woods, not knowing
what I'll find, not certain that I'll like it,
yet sure it doesn't matter, almost sure
I want to follow her into her world.

Frozen Over

Though the reservoir has frozen over,
no fishermen have ventured out to drill
their holes, plumb the bottom. The ice is still
finding its place, relieving pent-up stress
by fracturing, the making of each crack
accompanied by a melancholy
low-pitched moan, always the sound of rending
the whole. The lake won't break up till spring.
Meanwhile, each unruptured sheet's a country
living in fragile peace with its neighbors,
sometimes splitting, a new boundary formed.
There you are standing at the edge, thinking
you have to decide whether to step out
into that world, but you already have.

Something Missing

—after Shelley

Two vast and trunkless legs of snow, two feet
dumped by the storm and two feet, ankles, calves
sculpted by someone at curbside, complete
with toes and nails, sign that even the "haves"
find something missing in themselves, torso,
head, neck, arms, hands, thighs and knees gone, leaving
the indecisive feet behind, or so
it seems, the rest of the body heaving
from its anchor, engaging the traffic
of the bustling world, unafraid to land
where it may, unwilling to remain stuck
in place staring across the desert sand
dreaming of distant lands, exotic things,
wishing it had been born a king of kings.

Hey John

I have come to the great sandbox again
with my tools, shoveling an ivy league
schooling into soft pedestrian crap,
raking the years spent managing money,
filling the pail with numbers as jumbled
as the words in your work, except to you,
maybe even to you, who've come again,
I see, to the great sandbox with your tools
to build a castle no one else can scale.
Furnish a room in the turret for me,
high in the sky overlooking the sea,
looking down on the moat you can never
keep from filling in. And remember this:
though you wall me out, I always come back.

I Wished

1.

To prove the Riemann conjecture, and thus
to celebrate the genius who loved primes,
who knew that something primal lurked in them,
to tease it out and show it to the world,
to know what's real and imaginary
in complex numbers, to make us marvel
that the zeta function can be expressed
as an infinite product over primes,
to show how to count the number of primes
less than a billion or a billion raised
to the billionth power, what it means to
be a non-trivial zero with real
part one-half, that to know this universe
is to see the elegance of a mind.

2.

To co-ordinate hands and eyes, not with
brush and oils, though who would not wish to paint
like Rembrandt, or swish, find nothing but net
like Jordan, but to grip it and swing, send
the dimpled ball three hundred fifty yards
splitting the fairway, cozy an iron
to five feet, then sink the putt center cut.
And flop a shot from rough so deep you can't
see the ball nestled in a hole, yet it
lands on the fringe and rolls to tap-in range.
Blast from a fried-egg lie in sand beneath
a bunker's lip, drain a double breaker
twenty-seven feet one inch, saving par.
Sunday, Butler Cabin, first green jacket.

3.

To eat a Thursday brown-bag lunch again,
egg-salad sandwich and coke, cross-legged
on the floor, Busch-Reisinger Museum,
as E. Power Biggs bows and positions
himself at the Flentrop, adjusts the stops,
launches hands alone, no feet, the first notes—
Bach's "Toccata and Fugue in D Minor"—
thirty years ago, and now at the world's
largest mechanical pipe organ, one
of just two sixty-four foot-pedal-stop
instruments, I begin the toccata
before a packed house in Sydney's Town Hall,
ease into the much longer fugue, and with
the standing O, fifteen minutes of fame.

Bipolar Fields

I'm not sure it's solar flares that swing your moods,
but I've learned the sun is largest when it
isn't there. When it slips behind the earth,
you ask if anything still burns. You watch
an age-old sky and say so many stars
have died, but you can't tell which are still
alive. Nor can I. Don't you feel an urge
to touch a thing and have it touch you back?
See the dogwoods by the pines? Go. Caress
their blood-brown leaves and feel them crumble
in your hands. Are you sure they're dying?
The sap must freeze and thaw before you'll know.
Must you wait for dawn to feel a warming glow?
Go breathe on the coals. Hear the spit of fire.

Not Yet

No, not when you haven't finished counting the new
wrinkled leaves unfolding the oak, taken
last year's sum, then swum that number of laps

in the granite-cold pool before easing into the hot tub
to watch wisps break away from the mothership
and your children cross their thresholds. Not until

you've heard the wind as wishfulness turns to deed.
No matter that your joints have become the first
to greet you in the morning, even before you slip

out of bed, or that you need bifocals for the paper,
hearing aids for the birds. You stay because you want to
know where the ocean will draw the world's waistline

in a hundred years, whether what's left of continents
will come together again or continue to drift apart.
Easy enough, you figure, since you already don't exist

in your former state. Yes, you'll accept the rest
as plastic and titanium, having tried them in your heart.
You just hope they get the brain's circuitboards right.

Biographical Note

Jim Tilley earned a doctorate in Physics from Harvard University. He retired in 2001 after a 25-year career in insurance and investment banking. He has won numerous prizes for his papers in actuarial science, finance, and investments, and recently received a Founder's Award from the International Insurance Society for his pioneering work in asset-liability management. This is his first book of poems. He resides with his wife in Bedford Corners, New York.

811.6 TIL
Tilley, Jim.
In confidence : poems